Stardust

MAGIC BY MOONLIGHT

Linda Chapman

Illustrated by Biz Hull

PUFFI

PUFFIN BOOKS

Published by the Penguin Group
Penguin Books Ltd, 80 Strand, London WC2R 0RL, England
Penguin Group (USA), Inc., 375 Hudson Street, New York, New York 10014, USA
Penguin Books Australia Ltd, 250 Camberwell Road, Camberwell, Victoria 3124, Australia
Penguin Books Canada Ltd, 10 Alcorn Avenue, Toronto, Ontario, Canada M4V 3B2
Penguin Books India (P) Ltd, 11 Community Centre, Panchsheel Park, New Delhi – 110 017, India
Penguin Group (NZ), cnr Airborne and Rosedale Roads, Albany, Auckland 1310, New Zealand
Penguin Books (South Africa) (Pty) Ltd, 24 Sturdee Avenue, Rosebank 2196, South Africa

Penguin Books Ltd, Registered Offices: 80 Strand, London WC2R 0RL, England

www.penguin.com

First published 2004

1

Text copyright © Linda Chapman, 2004
Illustrations copyright © Biz Hull, 2004
All rights reserved

British Library Cataloguing in Publication Data
A CIP catalogue record for this book is available from the British Library

ISBN 0-141-31779-5

To Philippa Milnes-Smith,

for believing in stardust as much as I do

One

Twitch, twitch. The baby rabbit's whiskers trembled. Hopping to a patch of clover, he started to nibble quickly, his dark eyes darting around.

Nine-year-old Lucy Evans crouched down by the side of his run. 'Hi, boy,' she said softly.

Thumper looked up. Seeing Lucy, he hopped over. Stopping by the wire, he sat

up on his hind legs. Lucy rubbed his soft chestnut-brown fur with one of her fingers. 'Did you like those carrots I brought you earlier?' she asked.

Thumper pushed the side of his head against her fingers in reply. Lucy smiled at his confidence. Ever since her dad had brought Thumper home, the baby rabbit had been nervous of everyone apart from her. But then animals usually liked her – even wild animals sometimes let her get close.

Standing up, Lucy lifted the lid off the run and carefully took the rabbit out. He cuddled against her chest and she kissed the top of his head. Her long wavy hair, the exact same colour as Thumper's coat, fell over her face. She blew it out of her eyes. 'I'll bring you another treat later,' she promised.

Thumper wriggled slightly and looked back at the run. Lucy understood. 'OK, I get it. You want to go down and hop round again, don't you?'

Thumper's nose twitched in agreement.

She put him back in the run and watched him scamper back to the clover. A wave of sadness washed over her. If only Olivia was there to watch him too. But Olivia, her old best friend and next-door neighbour, had moved away three weeks ago. Lucy missed her lots. Her two sisters – twelve-year-old Rachel and thirteen-year-old Hope – hardly ever wanted her hanging round with them and it was lonely without a best friend. Particularly now it was the Easter holidays.

Maybe someone my age will move in next

door, Lucy thought, looking at the brick wall that separated her house, Jasmine Cottage, from Willow Cottage, the house next door. Willow Cottage had been empty since Olivia's family left but now it looked like someone had finally moved in. In the last few days there had been lots of people coming and going – mainly removal men and painters and decorators.

Lucy sighed. She hoped that whoever moved in was going to be nice.

Thumper was nibbling the clover. Not wanting to disturb him while he looked so happy, Lucy wandered around, trying to think of something to do. Her garden was long and winding with overgrown trees and bushes that were brilliant for climbing and hiding behind. At the end there was a gurgling stream and then fields and woods.

Lucy loved the woods. She and Olivia had played at the edges of them, making up games where they were fairies. They'd had to promise not to go too far into the trees though. The woods were very old and stretched for miles and miles.

'If you wander off in there we'd never find you,' Mrs Evans, Lucy's mum, often said.

Lucy looked at the woods now. The tall trees almost seemed to beckon her. What would it be like to go into them – deep, deep into them? What would she discover there?

'Hello!'

Lucy jumped and swung round.

To her surprise she saw a girl looking over the wall. She had medium-length, curly blonde hair and impish blue eyes that seemed to twinkle with fun. 'Do you live here?' she called.

Lucy nodded. 'Who are you?' she said, going over to the wall.

'My name's Allegra,' the girl replied. 'My

mum and I have just moved in. Can I come over into your garden?' Without waiting for Lucy to reply, she began to climb over the wall. She was skinny and slightly smaller than Lucy. 'What's your name and how old are you?' she asked, jumping down from the wall, her blonde curls bouncing on her shoulders.

'Lucy,' Lucy replied. 'And I'm nine.'

'Like me.' Allegra grinned. 'We can be friends.'

Her grin was infectious and Lucy found herself smiling back.

'Your garden's nice,' Allegra said, looking around curiously. She didn't seem the slightest bit shy. 'I love having the woods so close, don't you?'

Lucy nodded. 'My sisters say the woods are boring but –'

'Boring! Woods couldn't ever be boring!'
Allegra exclaimed, looking astonished.
'Woods are amazing and . . .' She broke
off. 'Oh wow!' she said, her eyes falling on
Thumper's run. 'You've got a rabbit!'

'Yes,' Lucy replied. 'He's called
Thumper. I got him just a few weeks ago.'

'Can I see him?' The words tumbled
out of Allegra's mouth. 'I love rabbits!'

Lucy nodded. 'He's quite nervous,' she
warned as she followed Allegra over to the
run. 'He doesn't usually let anyone but me
pick him up. He's only a baby.'

'He's gorgeous!' Allegra breathed. She
crouched down beside the wire. 'Hello,
Thumper.'

Thumper looked up and stared at
Allegra. Then to Lucy's utter surprise, he
hopped over and pressed his twitching

nose to the wire. Allegra tickled the fur on his nose and he stood up on his back legs, almost as if he were trying to get closer to her.

Lucy was amazed. 'He never usually does that with anyone apart from me!' She stared at Allegra. 'He's really scared of people.'

Allegra shrugged. 'Animals like me.'

'Me too,' Lucy said, suddenly feeling excited. 'Even wild animals.' Hope rushed through her. She and Allegra seemed really similar. Maybe they were going to be friends? Perhaps even best friends?

Allegra jumped to her feet, her blue eyes sparkling, and Lucy had the feeling she was thinking the same thing. 'Do you want to come and see my bedroom? My mum's just painted it.'

'OK,' Lucy agreed eagerly.

'Come on then!' Allegra said, running to the wall.

'We could go round by the path,' Lucy said, going after her.

Allegra grinned at her mischievously. 'Boring! It's much more fun to climb!'

Lucy had never tried climbing the wall before. It was quite high but surprisingly easy as long as you kept out of the way of the white climbing rose and its thorns. She landed in the garden on the long over-grown grass. Olivia's parents had built a section of wooden decking that extended out from the house, which they'd used to have drinks on in the summer. A woman was standing on the decking, shaking out a large brightly coloured throw. She was wearing a floaty purple skirt with little mirrors in the hem that twinkled as they caught the sun. Young and pretty, she had the same blonde curly hair as Allegra, except hers came halfway down her back and was held back with a lilac scarf.

'Xanthe, this is Lucy,' Allegra called to her. She turned to Lucy. 'Lucy, this is my mum, Xanthe.'

Lucy had never heard anyone call their mum by their first name before. She felt a bit awkward. 'Hello,' she said shyly.

'Lucy's come to see my bedroom,' Allegra told Xanthe. 'Have we got any biscuits? I'm starving.'

'I think there's some in a bag in the kitchen,' Xanthe said cheerfully. 'If you can find any you're welcome to them.'

'Do you always call your mum Xanthe?' Lucy asked as she followed Allegra inside.

There were unpacked boxes and bags everywhere.

Allegra nodded as she unearthed a packet of Hobnobs from the bottom of a plastic bag in the kitchen. 'I've never called her Mum. It would seem really weird.'

'What about your dad?' Lucy asked curiously. 'What do you call him?'

'I haven't got a dad,' Allegra replied, offering her a biscuit. 'Well, I mean I have,' she went on casually, 'but I've never met him. He left Xanthe when she found out she was pregnant with me.'

Lucy felt really embarrassed. 'That's awful,' she muttered, not knowing quite what to say.

Allegra shrugged. 'It's no big deal.' She threw down the packet of biscuits. 'Come on, let's go upstairs. I want to show you my room.'

Lucy followed her up the stairs and into one of the bedrooms. 'Oh wow!' she gasped. The walls were painted in different shades of lilac, pink and blue. White floaty curtains hung at the windows and there was a fluffy pink rug on the floor. But it wasn't those things that made Lucy gasp most. It was the ceiling. It was dark blue and painted to look like the sky at night. Lucy stared at it in wonder.

'Do you like it?' Allegra asked, and for the first time since Lucy had met her she sounded almost shy.

'I love it,' Lucy breathed. She turned and caught a look of relief crossing Allegra's face.

'Xanthe painted it so it looks exactly

like the sky looks at midnight on my birthday.' Allegra pointed at the ceiling. 'Look, you can see the different groups of stars. They're called constellations. Each constellation makes a different shape. If you look right above us you can see the shape of a big bear and a little bear.' She traced a pattern in the air. 'And over there you can see a dragon, and a harp.'

Lucy was fascinated. She had always loved looking up at the sky at night. 'You know loads,' she said, impressed.

'Xanthe's really into the stars,' Allegra said. 'She's taught me all about it. Some of the stars have names. You see that big one?' She pointed to a star to the left of the room. Lucy nodded. 'That's called Regulus. It's one of the four Royal Stars.'

'Royal Stars? What are they?' Lucy

asked curiously, sitting down on the bed.

'They're four of the brightest stars in the sky. In ancient times each of them used to shine out at the start of a new season and so they were called the Royal Stars,' Allegra explained. 'Regulus is the summer star. And that star over there,' she pointed to another very big star, 'is Antares, the autumn star. There are winter and spring stars too.'

Just then, Xanthe knocked on the door. 'Lucy,' she said. 'I've just heard your mum calling for you in your garden. Does she know you're here?'

Lucy jumped guiltily off the bed. 'No.'

'Then you'd better hurry back,' Xanthe advised.

Lucy didn't want to leave. She was having much too good a time.

'You can come back later,' Xanthe said, seeming to sense her reluctance.

'You could sleep over,' Allegra said. She glanced at Xanthe. 'That's all right, isn't it, Xanthe?'

'Of course,' Xanthe said. 'If the weather stays nice we'll eat supper outside on the deck.'

'OK,' Lucy said in delight. 'I'll ask.'

She hurried down the stairs feeling very excited. Life was suddenly looking much better indeed!

CHAPTER

Two

'Lucy, where have you been?' Mrs Evans exclaimed as Lucy ran into the kitchen. 'I've been looking for you everywhere.'

'I was just next door,' Lucy said, her greeny-grey eyes shining. 'These new people have moved in. Xanthe's Allegra's mum — Allegra's the girl and she's the same age as me. She's —'

'Lucy!' her mum interrupted. 'I can't

believe you went next door without telling me. I don't even know these people.'

'But they're really nice . . .' Lucy protested.

'Even so, you must never go off without telling me where you are. Do you understand?' Mrs Evans's voice was serious.

'Yes, Mum,' Lucy said patiently.

Mrs Evans looked slightly less annoyed. 'I was just worried, love.'

'I'm sorry,' Lucy said. She bit her lip. Was now the time to ask? She had to. She couldn't hold the question in any longer. The words burst out of her. 'Allegra's asked me to stay over tonight. Can I? Please?'

'Stay over?' Mrs Evans stared in surprise. 'But you've only just met and I haven't even been round to introduce myself.'

'So?' Lucy said impatiently. 'Go round now.' She looked pleadingly at her mum. 'Please, Mum!'

Mrs Evans looked at her for a moment and then gave in. 'OK, then,' she said smiling, half in exasperation. 'I can see I'm not going to get any peace until I do.'

Xanthe opened the front door of Willow Cottage.

'Xanthe, this is my mum,' Lucy said excitedly.

Xanthe smiled at Mrs Evans. 'Hello.' She held out her hand. 'Xanthe Greenwood and this,' she said as Allegra hurried forward, 'is my daughter, Allegra.'

'Carol Evans,' Lucy's mum said, shaking hands. Lucy saw her mum take in Xanthe's mirrored skirt and scarf. They were nothing like the sensible clothes her mum usually wore.

'Would you like to come in for a cup of tea?' Xanthe asked.

To Lucy's relief, her mum smiled. 'Thank you. That would be very nice.'

Any hope that Lucy had that her mum and Xanthe would become best friends quickly vanished. Drinking tea together, the two mums were polite but it was clear that after the initial getting to know you questions and talk about the village they had little to say to each other. For a start they had very different jobs. Mrs Evans was a maths teacher at a girls' secondary school and Xanthe was a reflexologist.

'Basically it means I massage and manipulate people's feet and hands to help with any problems they have,' Xanthe explained. 'The feet and hands are like maps of our body and through working on them it's possible to clear channels of blocked energy. Reflexology is all about helping the body to heal itself.'

Lucy was fascinated but she could tell that her mum, who was very practical and down to earth, thought that reflexology sounded a bit strange.

The conversation petered out and Mrs Evans stood up to go.

'Well, thank you very much for the tea, Xanthe, but I guess I'd better be getting home now. Come along, Lucy.'

Lucy stood up. She wanted to ask about staying over that night. Was her mum going to let her? While their mums had been talking, she and Allegra had been whispering together about their favourite animals and Lucy wanted to stay more than ever. However, she didn't quite dare ask in case the answer was no.

To her delight, Xanthe asked for her as they reached the door. 'Allegra would love it if Lucy could stay over tonight. Is that OK, Carol?'

Lucy saw her mum hesitate but then smile. 'That's fine.' Lucy felt a rush of relief. 'What time should she come over?'

'How about six o'clock?' Xanthe said. 'Then they can have tea together.'

Mrs Evans nodded. 'I'll bring Lucy over then.'

'So what did you think of them?' Lucy demanded as she and her mum went back into their house.

'They seem very nice,' Mrs Evans said cautiously. 'A bit alternative though. I've never met a reflexologist before and I'm not sure about Allegra calling her mother by her first name like that. Still, I guess different people have different ways.' She quickly changed the subject. 'Anyway, I'm sure you'll have a lovely time tonight. Why don't you go and get your pyjamas and toothbrush ready?'

Lucy hurried upstairs. She could tell her mum wasn't too sure about their new next-door neighbours. But she didn't care. She was going to stay with Allegra that night and that was all that mattered.

It was a brilliant evening. As soon as Lucy had put her bag in Allegra's room, Allegra dragged her down to the kitchen. 'Come

on, let's go and make some fairy cakes and
lemonade!'

It sounded great fun but Lucy felt a bit
concerned. 'Won't your mum mind?' she
said. At home she wasn't allowed to cook
in the evening. 'What if we make a mess?'

Allegra grinned. 'Xanthe never minds
about things like that. Come on. Fairy
cakes are easy but I bet you've never made
fairy lemonade before!'

Lucy hadn't. It seemed to have a bit of
everything in it – Allegra got out a jug of
home-made lemonade and added elder-
flower cordial, blackcurrant juice, a little
cranberry juice, a massive spoonful of
vanilla ice cream and then she gave it all a
stir round and poured it into two glasses.
She finished by sprinkling some tiny silver
sugar stars on the top of each glass. 'Try it.

It's delicious!' she said.

It was. They drank it as they chatted and made cakes. Once the cakes were cooked and had cooled they covered them in thick pink icing and more sugar stars. They looked great!

Afterwards they had supper with Xanthe on the raised wooden decking at the back of the house.

'I hope you don't mind vegetarian food,' she said to Lucy as they set out some cushions and a brightly checked cloth on the decking. 'Allegra and I don't eat meat.'

'That's fine,' Lucy said politely, but inside she was a bit worried. She didn't really like unusual things to eat. What if she hated the food?

She needn't have worried. It was all

delicious. Xanthe set out five different vegetarian dips and plates of organic crisps, breadsticks, carrots and cucumber to scoop up the dips with. There was also warm bread straight out of the oven, cheese and lots of butter.

'This is really nice,' Lucy said as they sat around cross-legged on the decking, munching their way through the food, giggling over silly jokes and watching the sun go down. It was strange having Xanthe sitting on the floor with them. It made her seem more like an older sister or friend than a mum.

At last, Xanthe sighed reluctantly. 'Well, I suppose I'd better get on with a bit more unpacking now. Help yourselves to ice cream.'

Allegra and Lucy got up and helped her

clear the plates away. Then they filled two
bowls with strawberry ice cream and went
outside again. The sun had disappeared
behind the horizon now and the first stars
were starting to twinkle in the dusky sky.

'Are those three stars part of a constellation?' Lucy asked, pointing out three
bright stars that seemed to shine in a
straight line.

Allegra nodded. 'They're part of Orion.
They're supposed to be his belt and sword.
Orion was a great hunter.' She waved her
spoon in the air. 'Look, you can just make
out his body and a leg and sort of a head,
although you have to look at the very
faint stars near the top of him.' She traced
the shape with her spoon. Lucy could just
about see it.

'Orion was killed by a scorpion who

stung his heel,' Allegra went on. 'You can sometimes see the scorpion on the other side of the sky.'

Lucy looked across. 'You won't see it now,' Allegra told her. 'Orion and the scorpion never share the sky. Orion goes as the scorpion comes. It's like he's always running away from it. Cool, isn't it?'

Lucy nodded. 'Very.'

Allegra propped herself up on her elbow and looked at Lucy almost quizzically for a moment. 'Have you ever dreamed of being up in the stars?' she said. 'Have you ever imagined flying in the sky at night, swooping through the trees?'

Lucy stared at her. Sometimes, before she went to sleep at night, she imagined being able to fly out of her bedroom window into the stars. But it was a

made-up game she hadn't even shared
with Olivia. 'Yes,' she said in surprise. 'Yes,
I have!'

Excitement flashed across Allegra's face.
Without warning, she leapt to her feet and
grabbed Lucy's hands. 'Let's pretend we
can do it,' she said, her eyes shining. 'Come
on, let's pretend we can fly like that.'

Lucy scrambled up. She loved playing
'let's pretend' games. 'OK! What shall we
do?'

'First we've got to make ourselves able
to fly,' Allegra said. 'There's only one way
to do that. We have to shut our eyes and
say, "I believe in stardust," three times. It's
stardust that makes you fly.'

Lucy felt a tingle of excitement. It
might be just a pretend game but there
was something very magical about being

outside under the stars, and the way Allegra was talking made it sound almost real.

'Are you ready?' Allegra said.

'Ready,' Lucy nodded.

She shut her eyes.

'You've got to really believe it when you say it,' Allegra told her. 'Really believe.' She took a deep breath and squeezed Lucy's hands. 'After three. One, two, three. I believe in stardust . . .'

'I believe in stardust,' Lucy whispered.

She screwed her eyes shut.

'I believe in stardust,' she said more strongly. Her body felt strange, as if it was dissolving, getting lighter. This was weird! Keeping her eyes tightly closed, she gasped, '*I believe in stardust!*'

Suddenly she felt a whooshing feeling.

The next second her body seemed to melt away. Her eyes snapped open. The ground was disappearing beneath her and she was shooting into the sky.

'I'm flying!' she cried.

She heard a giggle and looked round. Allegra was in the air beside her, only she was half the size that she had been and her jeans and jumper had disappeared. She was now wearing a shining silver dress and every inch of her skin and hair seemed to sparkle and glow.

'What . . . what's happening?' gasped Lucy, staring at her in astonishment.

Allegra grinned at her in delight. 'You're a stardust spirit!' she said.

CHAPTER

Three

Lucy stared at Allegra. 'I . . . I'm a what?'

'A stardust spirit,' Allegra said.

'What's a stardust spirit?' Lucy
stammered, almost too shocked to speak.
Looking down, she saw that the ground
was a very long way away. *I'm flying!* The
thought spun round in her mind like a
Catherine wheel.

'A stardust spirit is a person who has

more stardust than other people,' Allegra replied. She seemed to see Lucy's look of total bewilderment. 'It's like this. Everyone is made out of stardust – every person in the world – but some people, like you and me, have more stardust than others. It means that when the sun sets we can turn into stardust spirits. All we have to do is say the magic words "I believe in stardust" three times and all the earthly bits of our bodies just melt away. We become pure stardust and we can fly!'

Lucy still couldn't take it in. She looked at her body. Her skin was sparkling and she was wearing a dress like Allegra's, only hers was a shimmering pearly grey. She shook her head. This *had* to be a dream.

Allegra saw her face and flew over to her. 'It's OK,' she said. 'I guess it can be a shock when it first happens. It wasn't for me, of course, but then I've always known I'm a stardust spirit – Xanthe's one too.'

'Your mum's a stardust spirit?' Lucy echoed.

Allegra nodded. 'We were sure you were a stardust spirit too. You can nearly always tell.'

Lucy's head spun. 'I'm a stardust spirit,' she said, as if repeating it would make her believe it. 'And I . . . I'm flying!'

'Well, technically you're just floating at the minute,' Allegra told her with a grin. '*This* is flying!' She shot through the air in a straight line, veered to the left, turned head over heels and raced back to Lucy.

'Wow!' Lucy said. 'How did you do that?' Excitement flickered through her, starting at her toes and gathering in

intensity until it was fizzing like sherbet
through her whole body. This was really
happening. She really *was* a stardust spirit!
'How do I fly like you?'

'You have to use your mind,' Allegra
answered. 'To go forward you have to
imagine that you are pushing the air
behind you. If you think it hard enough it
will happen. To go left you push the air to
your right and to go right you push the air
to your left. It takes a bit of concentration
at first but soon it'll seem really easy. Have
a go!'

Lucy thought about the air in front of
her and tried to imagine pushing it back.
She began to move very slowly forward.
'I'm doing it!' she gasped.

Allegra giggled. 'You need to go faster
than that. Here.' She grabbed Lucy's hand.

'Try again and I'll do it with you!'

Push back, push back, Lucy thought. The next instant she was shooting across the sky with Allegra. She gasped in astonishment as the stars flew by. 'I'm flying!'

'It's fun, isn't it?' Allegra said. She let go of Lucy's hand and turned a pirouette. 'Try again.'

Soon, Lucy was shooting about on her own. She was nowhere near as expert as Allegra, who seemed to be able to dance through the air as lightly as thistledown but she could at least go forward and backwards and sideways – and she could go fast!

'This is brilliant!' she cried as they swooped through the sky, holding hands together. She saw the roof of her house. 'I can't wait to tell Mum and Dad!'

'But you can't tell them,' Allegra said quickly. 'For a start, they won't believe you, they'll think you're making it up, and anyway, stardust spirits have to stay secret. Other people can't know. They mustn't.'

Lucy felt a flash of disappointment but it quickly disappeared as Allegra pulled her into a steep dive. 'Wow!' she cried as the wind whipped her cheeks.

'You think that's fun?' Allegra said. 'Watch this!'

Letting go of Lucy's hand, she flew a little bit away and muttered a word. Suddenly she disappeared.

Lucy stared. One second she'd been there, the next she'd gone. Where was she? 'Allegra?' she called, looking all around in bewilderment.

'I'm here!'

Lucy could hear Allegra's voice but she couldn't see her. 'Are you invisible?' she gasped.

'Not totally,' Allegra's voice came back. 'Look hard and see if you can spot me.'

Lucy looked in the direction of the voice. There was a faint shimmering in the air. She frowned. Was that Allegra? She flew over cautiously and reached out. Her hand touched soft fabric and the next minute Allegra was flying and laughing beside her. Lucy was touching her dress.

'It's called camouflaging,' Allegra said seeing Lucy's astonished expression. 'You see the way our skin shimmers? Well, we can use that to disguise ourselves against things so that we can hardly be seen. You have a try. All you have to do is imagine yourself the same colour as the back-

ground and say "Camouflagus". Try down
here.' They flew down to the garden and
landed on the grass.

Lucy hurried over to the wooden shed.
'Camouflagus,' she whispered. She felt a
strange tickling sensation as if tiny stars
were twinkling all over her skin. She
looked down. There was just a faint
shimmering in the air where her body
had been.

'That's really good,' Allegra said
approvingly. 'And if you keep moving
you'll be almost impossible to see.'

For the next hour they charged about
the garden taking it in turns to hide by
camouflaging themselves. Lucy had never
had such fun.

'You're a fast learner,' Allegra told her. 'I
bet you're going to end up being a really

powerful stardust spirit.'

Lucy grinned in delight.

'Come on,' Allegra said, swooping away in a smooth easy movement. 'Let's go and tell Xanthe about you.'

They flew down to the house. When they landed on the deck, Allegra showed Lucy how to turn back to her human self by saying, 'Stardust be gone,' three times.

Dressed once again in their jeans and jumpers they hurried indoors. Xanthe was in the kitchen, setting out a row of herbs on the window sill. She turned as they came in, her eyes looking questioningly at Allegra.

Allegra nodded. 'We were right. Lucy *is* a stardust spirit!'

Xanthe's face lit up in delight. 'That's wonderful!' She stepped forward and hugged Lucy. 'I was sure you were, Lucy. There's a glow about people who are stardust spirits. They're also more imaginative than most people, more in tune with animals and nature and magic. You seemed just the type.' She looked closely at Lucy. 'So how are you feeling?'

'Amazed!' Lucy admitted. 'I never even knew there were such things as stardust spirits. But it's wonderful.'

'So are you looking forward to starting your stardust work?' Xanthe said eagerly.

Lucy looked at her in surprise. 'Work? What work?'

'Your work as a stardust spirit,' Xanthe said. 'Hasn't Allegra told you about that?'

Allegra grinned. 'We've been having too much fun flying!'

Xanthe smiled. 'I can imagine.' She

turned to Lucy. 'Well, although flying's fun, stardust spirits aren't here just to swoop round. We have a job to do. We have to look after the natural world.'

'Xanthe means birds and plants and animals,' Allegra put in.

Xanthe nodded. 'Humans can be very destructive towards nature. Our job is to right the wrongs they do. All over the world, stardust spirits meet in woods and forests and watch out for disturbances caused by humans. Our work can be as simple as freeing a swan with a fishing hook caught in its beak or as complex as protecting a species threatened with extinction because of man's activities. We repair damage, we watch over and we protect. That's what our magic powers are for.'

'Magic powers!' Lucy said, her eyes widening. 'What magic powers?'

'As a stardust spirit you will have certain magical powers,' Xanthe told her. 'The powers you'll have will depend on what type of stardust spirit you are. Some stardust spirits can make things grow, others can conjure winds or rain or warmth.'

'There are four types of stardust spirit,' Allegra put in. 'Winter spirits, spring spirits, summer spirits and autumn spirits.'

'What type am I?' Lucy asked eagerly. She loved the thought of having magic powers.

'We can't tell you,' Xanthe said. 'Each stardust spirit has to discover their powers for themselves. It will depend on which Royal Star your stardust comes from – Aldebaran the spring star, Regulus the

summer star, Antares the autumn star or
Fomalhaut the winter star. Every stardust
spirit's stardust comes from one of those
four stars but only *you* can find out which
star is yours.'

Lucy put her hands to her face. Her
thoughts were spinning.

Xanthe squeezed her shoulder gently.
'I think you've probably had enough
information for tonight, Lucy,' she said
softly. 'Look, it's past midnight. Why don't
you two go to bed now? There will be
plenty of nights to come when you can
discover more.'

Lucy felt torn. She wanted to find out
more – to find out everything – but her
head was in such a whirl she could hardly
think straight. 'OK,' she agreed.

She followed Allegra up to her bedroom. They brushed their teeth and got into their pyjamas. Xanthe had set out a camp bed beside Allegra's bed.

'Tomorrow night we'll have loads of fun. We'll go to the woods,' Allegra said as they climbed into bed. 'There's so much to see and do there. You'll get to meet every-one too.'

'You mean other stardust spirits?' Lucy asked eagerly.

'Yes,' Allegra replied. She yawned and turned off the light. 'Night then.'

'Night,' Lucy said. She lay back in the darkness. *I'm a stardust spirit,* she thought, hugging herself in delight. *I can fly.*

Through Allegra's open curtains she could see the stars twinkling in the night sky. She remembered what Xanthe had said about each stardust spirit belonging to a star.

I wonder, she thought with a flash of excitement, *which star is mine?*

CHAPTER

Four

When Lucy went home after breakfast the next morning she felt like every bit of her body was buzzing with her news. She didn't know how she was ever going to keep quiet about it.

As she went up the path to the back door she saw that Mum and Dad were in the kitchen together tidying up their breakfast dishes.

'Hi! I'm home!' Lucy exclaimed, pushing the door open.

'Hi, sweetheart,' her dad said warmly. 'How was your sleepover?'

'Brilliant!' Lucy replied, her eyes glowing. 'Just brilliant!'

'So you got on all right with Allegra?' her mum asked. 'You still like her?'

Lucy nodded. 'We had the best time!'

'What did you get up to?' Mrs Evans asked.

Lucy longed to tell her but she knew she couldn't. 'We made fairy cakes and fairy lemonade,' she said, telling part of the truth. 'And then we ate outside on the deck. We had a picnic – Allegra and Xanthe are vegetarians but I really liked the food.'

Just then, Rachel, Lucy's twelve-year-old sister, came into the kitchen. She was still in her dressing gown. 'Morning,' she yawned sleepily. She headed over to the bread bin and got out a piece of bread. 'So what are the neighbours like then, Luce?' she said as she put the bread in the toaster.

'Really nice,' Lucy replied.

'It sounds like you had a good time,' Robert Evans said, looking affectionately at his youngest daughter. 'Having fairy feasts and things.'

Rachel raised her eyebrows mockingly. 'So you've found another little friend who likes playing "let's pretend" magic games, have you, Lucy?'

Lucy glared at her. Rachel was always teasing her for liking fairies and magic.

'Oh, Rachel,' Mrs Evans sighed wearily. 'Don't start winding your sister up already.'

Rachel ignored her and grinned at Lucy. 'Does she believe in magic too? Does she think fairies are real?'

Lucy only just managed to keep her temper. If only Rachel knew! 'Mum,' she said, turning her back on her annoying older sister. 'Allegra's asked me if I want to sleep over again tonight. Can I?'

Mrs Evans looked surprised. 'Sleep over again already?' She shook her head. 'No, not tonight, love. Maybe in a few days.'

Lucy stared at her. She hadn't expected her to say no. 'But, Mum! Why not?'

'You've only just become friends,' Mrs Evans said. 'It's a bit soon to be sleeping over every night.'

Lucy thought about the trip to the woods she and Allegra had planned for that evening and her voice rose. 'But I've

got to stay over. You don't understand. I
need to.'

Her mum smiled. 'Oh, Lucy. Why do
you always exaggerate? I hardly think you
need to.' Her voice was firm. 'No. Allegra
can come round and play today but I want
you to stay here tonight.'

Lucy looked at her dad but, as always,
he nodded in agreement with her mum.
Feeling her heart sink, Lucy realized there
was no point in arguing any more.

'What am I going to do?' Lucy
whispered to Allegra later that morning.
'If I can't stay with you we can't go to
the woods.'

'Yes, we can,' Allegra said, as they
walked to the bottom of Lucy's garden
together. 'We just have to wait till your

mum and dad are asleep. What time do
they go to bed?'

'About ten thirty,' Lucy replied.

'Well, turn yourself into a stardust spirit
then and come to mine. We can fly to the
woods. Nothing need change.'

'OK,' Lucy said in excitement.

Allegra grinned. 'You're going to have
such a good time tonight. Just wait and
see!'

Lucy was desperate to ask Allegra more
about the stardust world but just as they
settled down in the garden to talk, her dad
came outside.

'Going to help me with the weeding?'
he asked, smiling at them.

'Not now, Dad,' Lucy replied hurriedly.

They went into the house but Rachel
was in the lounge watching TV and Hope

was in the kitchen.

'Let's go to my room,' Lucy suggested,
but her mum was upstairs doing the
hoovering.

'We'll talk tonight,' Allegra whispered as
they went back downstairs.

Lucy nodded. She felt very frustrated.
There were so many questions she wanted
to ask!

As evening fell, Lucy found herself
watching the clock. By eight o'clock she
was pacing round her bedroom. Soon she
would get to be a stardust spirit again. She
went to the window sill and looked out at
the darkening sky. In just a few hours she
would be flying across the sky. She hugged
herself in excitement. She remembered the
feeling of the wind in her face, the stars

flashing above her. She couldn't wait!

At nine o'clock she got into bed and turned her light out. She listened to the sounds downstairs. She really hoped her parents wouldn't stay up late. The clock hands slowly ticked round and each minute seemed to take an hour. She heard

Rachel and Hope go to bed and then, at long last, her mum and dad came upstairs. She lay still and shut her eyes. Her bedroom door opened. She knew her mum was looking in.

There was a second's pause and then the door shut again.

Lucy breathed out in relief. She'd been sure her mum would guess she wasn't really asleep.

There were the sounds of her parents brushing their teeth and going into their bedroom and then finally all was quiet.

Lucy forced herself to wait ten minutes more and then she got out of bed and tiptoed to the window. The stars shone down at her from the black sky. She opened the window as quietly as she could. A gust of cold night air blew in and she shivered slightly.

Suddenly she felt a flicker of doubt. This was going to work, wasn't it?

Yes, she told herself firmly. *Yes, it will.*

She heard Allegra's voice from the night before. *You've got to really believe.*

Taking a deep breath Lucy shut her eyes. 'I believe in stardust,' she whispered. 'I believe in stardust.' She felt a tingling sensation run through her as if she was getting lighter. '*I believe in stardust!*' she gasped and the next second her body seemed to melt away.

She only just stopped herself from crying out in delight as she whooshed up into the air. It had happened. She was flying again.

She hovered near the ceiling of her bedroom. She no longer felt cold – in fact, her whole body seemed to glow. She felt as warm as if she was outside on a summer's day.

She tried to remember how to fly. Pushing the air back with her mind she flew to the window. It was open just enough for her to get out. Excitement racing through her, she dived out into the starry sky.

Five

'This way!' Allegra said. She had been waiting by her bedroom window. As soon as she'd seen Lucy she had flown out to join her.

It was dark but Lucy realized she could see perfectly. She wondered if it was more stardust magic.

'Where's Xanthe?' she asked Allegra as they swooped across the fields behind their houses and towards the woods.

'Still at home,' Allegra said. 'She'll come later. I don't see that much of her when I'm a stardust spirit. She stays with the grown-ups and I stay with my friends.'

'Friends?' Lucy said in surprise. It hadn't occurred to her that Allegra might have other stardust friends.

'Yes,' Allegra replied. 'My best friends are Ella and Faye.' She smiled. 'You're going to really like them, Luce.'

Lucy felt a strange feeling almost like jealousy. Allegra had two best friends already. But she'd thought *she* was Allegra's best friend.

'Come on!' Allegra said impatiently. 'I can't wait for you to meet them!'

★

'Where do we go?' Lucy called as they flew into the woods. She was getting much better at flying but she still had to really concentrate to go fast and Allegra kept shooting on ahead of her.

'We're going to the secret glade,' Allegra replied, stopping and spinning on the spot like a ballet dancer. 'Every wood has a hidden clearing right in its centre, usually by the oldest tree. It's called the secret glade and it's where stardust spirits meet at night.'

The wood was enormous. At long last, Allegra called, 'Here we are!' She swooped down between the trees.

Lucy followed her and gasped. In the very centre of the woods, there was a large circle of grass and standing or flying around it were about thirty stardust spirits,

their clothes shimmering in shades of
gold, silver, blue and green.

Allegra waved to two of the youngest
stardust spirits who were playing a game
of tag in the sky. 'Ella! Faye!' Allegra called
excitedly. 'Over here!'

The two girls stopped flying and looked
round. Seeing Allegra their faces broke
into smiles and they flew over. One was
wearing a sky-blue dress that sparkled as if
covered by a thousand tiny sapphires and
the other had a green dress that glowed
and rippled like spring leaves on an oak
tree.

'Hi, Allegra!' the girl in the green dress
said. She looked curiously at Lucy. She was
the taller of the two girls. Her eyes were
brown and her long black hair was caught
back in a ponytail with a green ribbon.

'This is Lucy,' Allegra explained. 'She's my new next-door neighbour and she just found out last night that she's a stardust spirit!'

'Cool!' the girl in the green dress said, smiling at Lucy. 'I'm Ella.'

'Hello, Lucy, I'm Faye,' the girl in the blue dress said more quietly. She had short fair hair, large blue eyes and a heart-shaped almost pixie-like face.

'Hi,' Lucy replied. She felt unusually shy. It was strange meeting other stardust spirits.

Faye seemed to guess how she was feeling. 'It's a bit weird when you find out you're a stardust spirit, isn't it?' she said softly. 'I found out three months ago and it took me ages to get used to the idea.'

'It's great fun though,' Ella said. 'You'll

love it!' She looked at Allegra. 'So what are
we going to do tonight?'

'I thought we could fly to the horse
chestnut glade in the north,' Allegra said
thoughtfully. 'Check that everything's OK
round there.' She looked at Lucy.
'Checking out the woods is what we do at
night. Powerful adult spirits like my mum
deal with any big problems or threats and
communicate with stardust spirits in other
woods. As for everyone else, well, it
depends on how well we can control our
magic. When we have proved we can use
our powers safely and work with other
stardust spirits we're allowed to explore
outside the woods and to use magic on
people. But until then we have to stay here
and look out for any problems.'

'We also have to learn about the stars

and about endangered plants and animals,'
Faye put in.

Allegra sighed longingly. 'I can't wait to
be good enough to be allowed to do
magic out of the woods.' Her blue eyes lit
up. 'Maybe we could go one night. No
one would know.'

'We can't,' Ella said firmly. 'You know
we're not allowed.'

Allegra grinned. 'So?'

Ella frowned but before she could
speak, Faye quickly burst in. 'Please don't
start arguing, you two. Let's go to the
chestnut glade.'

Allegra rose up into the air. 'All right
then. Come on!'

Ella and Faye flew up into the air beside
her and Lucy quickly followed them. As
they swooped out of the clearing, Lucy

was relieved to find out that she wasn't the only one who couldn't match Allegra's speed and skill at flying. Ella and Faye seemed to have trouble too.

'Wait for us, Allegra!' Ella called. She glanced at Lucy. 'It's a nightmare keeping up with Allegra. It's because she's an autumn spirit. Autumn spirits can always fly really well.'

An autumn spirit! Lucy wanted to ask more but she was concentrating too hard on keeping up.

After ten minutes, they reached a glade of sweet chestnut trees.

'You two search over there. Lucy and I will look here,' Allegra instructed bossily as they flew down. She seemed to be the leader of the little group. 'If you need help, call out!'

Ella and Faye nodded and flew off into the shadow of the trees together.

Allegra turned to grin at Lucy. 'So what do you think of Ella and Faye? They're nice, aren't they?'

'Yeah,' Lucy replied. 'Really nice.' She meant it — they did seem nice — but there was a tiny bit of her that was glad it was only her and Allegra now, just like it had been the night before.

They landed among the trees. 'What are we looking for?' she asked.

'Just for anything that doesn't seem right,' Allegra replied vaguely.

They started to explore. Suddenly Allegra hissed, 'Listen!'

Lucy listened hard and heard the faintest of scrabbling noises. It sounded like tiny nails scratching against metal.

Allegra stood very still and looked round. 'There!' she said suddenly. She pointed towards a pile of leaves. They were moving slightly.

Allegra hurried forward. Lucy watched her crouch down and gently start to move leaves from the pile. An empty drinks can appeared. It was shaking slightly and as Allegra moved the leaves from around it Lucy saw the reason why.

A tiny brown shrew had obviously decided to investigate the can and it had got its head trapped inside. It was scrab-bling at the metal with its front paws. Its body was shaking.

'Hush,' Allegra whispered, placing her hands gently on its tiny body. As soon as it heard her voice and felt her touch it seemed to relax. 'Lucy,' Allegra said without looking round. 'Can you come and help me?'

Lucy hurried over and knelt beside her.

'If you can push the metal back a little bit I think I'll be able to wriggle him out,' Allegra said. 'Stay still,' she soothed to the shrew.

Lucy saw what was needed. If the hole was just slightly bigger the shrew, if it stayed calm, would be able to slip his head out. She pushed her thumbs against the edges of the hole in the can. The metal gave slightly.

'That's it!' Allegra said and she gently eased the shrew out. The second he was out he shook his brown head as if unable to believe he was free.

Allegra held him in her cupped hands. 'Don't go doing that again,' she told him.

He sat up on her palms and looked at her, his whiskers twitching, his black eyes relieved.

'Go on,' Allegra whispered. 'Off you go!' She put him down and with a squeak he bounded away across the forest floor. 'Litter!' she said, shaking her head as she picked up the can. 'Why can't people put it in a bin?'

Lucy didn't answer. She was very impressed with what she had just seen. 'He seemed to know you were helping him,' she said. 'Did he understand you? Can stardust spirits talk to animals?'

'Not exactly,' Allegra replied. 'Animals know we aren't going to hurt them and so most of the time they trust us. That's why the shrew stayed still.' She put the can into the pocket of her dress and then flew up into the air. 'Come on, let's go and tell the others!'

As they flew across the trees Lucy heard a noise that made her slow down. It was a frightened chirruping noise. 'What's that?'

'I don't know,' Allegra said. 'Let's go and see.'

'Oh poor thing!' Lucy cried softly as

they flew lower. A fledgling bird had fallen from its nest and was lying injured on the forest floor. Lucy's eyes caught a flash of russet in the trees. It was a fox! He was trotting towards the baby bird.

Not stopping to think, Lucy swooped downwards. But all of a sudden she found herself jerking upright.

Allegra had grabbed hold of her left arm. 'No!'

Lucy tried to shake her off. 'What are you doing?' she cried. 'Quick! The poor bird!'

It was too late. Under Lucy's horrified gaze, the fox pounced on the bird and in one swift mouthful the fledgling was gone.

'Allegra!' Lucy exclaimed, hot anger pumping through her blood. 'Why did you stop me? I could have saved it!'

'That's not our job!' As the fox slunk away into the bushes, Allegra sighed and let go of Lucy's arm. 'We can't interfere with nature, Lucy. It's one of the main rules of being a stardust spirit.'

Lucy felt her fury fade to be replaced by a feeling of confusion. 'What . . . what do you mean?'

'We can help animals and plants that are in distress because of humans,' Allegra explained. 'But we can't stop things that are natural, like one animal killing another. If we stopped the fox killing then it would starve itself. We mustn't interfere.'

'Oh,' Lucy said. She guessed she could see the sense in what Allegra was saying but she didn't really like it.

'I know it's hard, but you'll get used to it in the end,' Allegra said quietly.

Feeling subdued, Lucy followed her as she flew back up into the sky.

Ella and Faye were on the other side of the glade. They were standing beside a very overgrown and tangly patch of brambles that rose up in the middle of the path like a small hill.

Faye was giggling. 'Ella! I told you not to try using magic. Now look what you've done.'

'It's not that bad,' Ella replied, considering the bramble bush sheepishly. 'And you've got to admit it's better than what was there before!'

Allegra landed beside them. 'OK, what's been going on?' she grinned.

Faye pointed at the bush. 'We found a patch of ground that people had been using for a campfire. It was all blackened

and the plants had been burnt away. I said
we should go and get help but Ella said
she could fix it herself. And now look!'

Allegra giggled. 'It's a bramble moun-
tain!'

'How did you do it?' Lucy asked, looking at the giant bramble bush in
amazement.

'With my powers,' Ella replied, as if it
was obvious.

'Ella's a spring spirit,' Allegra explained.
'Her stardust comes from the spring star,
Aldebaran. It means that she has the
powers to make things grow and it's why
her dress is green. All spring spirits have
green clothes.'

Lucy stared at her. 'So the colour of
your dress depends on the type of spirit
you are.'

'Exactly,' Allegra replied. 'When you find out what your star is your dress will change to either silver, blue, green or gold. My dress is silver because I'm an autumn spirit. I can control the wind – well, supposedly,' she added.

'None of us are very good at controlling our powers yet,' Faye admitted. 'I'm a winter spirit and I know I can summon rain and snow but I just can't work out how to do it properly. Sometimes I get drizzle and sometimes a snowstorm. Look.' She held out her hands and concentrated hard on them. 'Rain!' she whispered, waving a hand at a nearby tree. 'Be with me!'

The next second, a black cloud appeared directly above them and rain came cascading down.

Lucy gasped as the cold water hit her.

'Faye!' Allegra shrieked.

Spluttering with surprise, Faye waved her hands from side to side. 'Water be gone!' she gasped.

The black cloud disappeared with a pop.

'Yuck!' Allegra cried, shaking herself like a dog. 'I'm soaked, Faye.'

'Sorry,' Faye said quickly. 'I meant it to go on that tree over there.'

Ella looked at Lucy. 'You see what we mean about not being able to control our powers properly.'

'Yeah,' Lucy grinned, pushing back her soaking wet hair. 'I see.'

'We're all useless,' Ella went on. 'But then all stardust spirits are to start with. We're supposed to practise and practise until we get better.'

Lucy felt very excited at the thought of having magic powers, even ones she couldn't control. 'I want to find out what powers I've got,' she said eagerly.

'Well, have a go at looking at the stars,' Faye suggested. 'See if one of them sort of calls to you. That's what I did. Fomalhaut, my star, just seemed to glow much brighter than all the rest to me and I knew as soon as I saw it that I must be a winter spirit.'

Heart beating fast with excitement, Lucy looked up. Was she actually going to discover what her powers were? She stared at the stars twinkling brightly overhead.

Call to me, she thought. *Tell me which one you are!*

CHAPTER
Six

'Well?' Faye asked.

'I . . . I don't know,' Lucy said uncertainly, looking up into the sky. 'There are quite a few bright stars.'

'But isn't there one that seems to call to you?' Faye said.

'No,' Lucy replied. She looked down, feeling a rush of disappointment. She desperately wanted to find out what her powers were.

'Try this instead. Which season do you like best?' Ella asked. 'Spring, summer, autumn, winter?'

Lucy thought for a moment. 'I . . . I like them all.'

The others looked at each other.

'I've got an idea,' Allegra suggested. 'Shut your eyes and see which power comes to you. Wind, water, growing things or heating things up. You have to really concentrate. If it works, you'll feel the power sort of flowing into you from the stars.'

Lucy shut her eyes and tried to concentrate. Wind, water, growing things or heat. They all flickered through her mind but no power flowed through her. She opened her eyes.

'Well?' Allegra asked eagerly.

'I didn't feel anything,' Lucy admitted in a small voice. She felt like she had failed.

'Don't worry,' Faye said quickly. 'It's normal, Lucy. It's only your second night as a stardust spirit. Sometimes it can take ages for spirits to find their powers.'

'Yes,' Ella agreed. 'It took me almost three weeks. Xanthe told me that sometimes the longer it takes, the more powerful a spirit you are.'

Lucy felt a bit better.

'Come on,' Allegra said. 'Let's go back to the clearing and find the others.'

They rose into the sky again. As they flew up through the branches of the horse chestnut trees, Lucy felt the wind on her face and her heart lifted. So what if she didn't know what her star was? She would find out soon enough. The stars flickered past her and she felt her skin sparkling and glowing. She was a stardust spirit. Nothing else mattered apart from that.

Xanthe was in the secret clearing. They sat on the grass around her and drank cups of sweet honey and chamomile lemonade, while she explained about another side of their job as stardust spirits.

'We need to concentrate on encouraging rare and endangered species back to the woods,' she told them. 'These woods used to hold lots of creatures and plants which have since disappeared because of humans – large blue butterflies, dormice, firecrests, even otters and great crested newts down by the river. If the habitats are protected, then the animals will return and when they

return we can help them to live happily.
Look after the woods and keep your eyes
open for signs that the animals are coming
back. A hazelnut shell with the nut nibbled
out of the centre might mean a dormouse
is living here, eggs laid on wild thyme
could be a sign of the large blue butterfly,
flattened reeds by the riverbank could be an
otter den.'

It was fascinating listening to everything
she had to say. By the end of half an
hour Lucy's mind was buzzing with
information. There was so much to
remember – but it was all so much fun!

At long last, Allegra and Lucy flew
home. They swooped through the air,
taking it in turns to camouflage themselves
and disappear. 'I'll see you tomorrow,
Luce,' Allegra whispered softly when they

reached their houses.

'Yeah, night!' Lucy smiled and she flew over the wall.

Landing in her bedroom, she whispered, 'Stardust be gone.' A sinking, heavy sensation swept over her as her body grew back to full size. And then suddenly she was standing in her pyjamas, shivering in the cold night air.

She quickly shut her window but paused as she drew her curtains. The stars twinkled down at her. Her eyes scanned the sky. Which one was hers? Which magic powers would she have?

I'll find out soon, she thought determinedly. *I know I will.*

The next day, Lucy couldn't stop smiling. She didn't think she'd ever felt happier in her entire life.

'What's up with you?' Rachel demanded after lunch as Lucy grinned all the way through washing the dishes.

'Nothing,' Lucy said blithely. 'I'm just feeling happy today!'

'You're weird,' Rachel said.

'Leave her alone,' Hope said. She was kinder than Rachel. 'What are you doing this afternoon, Lucy? If you want you can hang round with us. We're not doing much today.'

Rachel shot Hope a horrified look. Tempting though it was to annoy her middle sister by saying yes to Hope's offer, Lucy shook her head. 'It's OK, thanks. I'm going round to Allegra's.'

Hope smiled. 'So you're still getting on really well with her then?'

'Really well,' Lucy said, brimming with happiness. 'She's my best friend!'

As soon as the dishes were done, Lucy went next door. She and Allegra played together all afternoon and then, that evening, she did just as she had done the night before. After waiting for her parents to go to bed, she turned into a stardust spirit and flew over to her friend's house.

'Let's go to the river tonight,' Allegra suggested when they met up with Ella and Faye in the clearing.

'Do you remember that time we found those trampled reeds and Ella tried to regrow them?' Faye said with a giggle.

Allegra laughed. 'That was brilliant!'

'What happened?' Lucy asked curiously.

'I used some magic and the reeds grew three metres high,' Ella explained. 'They were gigantic!'

'One of the adults had to come and shrink them back down,' Allegra chuckled. 'It was very funny!'

'We've had some brilliant nights, haven't we?' Ella said to her. 'Remember the time you knocked a tree down with that wind, Allegra?'

Allegra nodded and grinned. 'And the time Faye made the river flood.'

Faye giggled. 'Your mum was really mad.'

'Still,' Allegra said. 'We haven't had any major disasters for ages. I think we're definitely getting better at using our powers.'

They started talking about some of the adventures they'd had in the past. At first it was interesting to listen to but gradually

Lucy began to feel more and more left out. Feeling bored, she began to wander away into the clearing.

'Where are you going, Lucy?' Allegra asked.

'Nowhere,' Lucy said quickly.

Faye smiled at her. 'Sorry, we've probably been really boring.'

'No,' Lucy lied, shaking her head. 'It's fine.'

Allegra rose into the air. 'We've talked enough. Let's go to the river!'

It was great to be flying again and, as they swooped through the trees, Lucy almost forgot about feeling like the odd one out.

She was getting much better at flying and when they reached the river she plunged downwards, planning to land in a spectacular dive, but Allegra caught up with her and grabbed her arm just before she landed.

Lucy gasped as she jerked to a sudden stop. 'What did you do that for?' she demanded.

'Sorry,' Allegra apologized. 'It's just you have to be careful when you land. There are sometimes adders in the undergrowth.'

'Adders?' Lucy said. She knew they were poisonous snakes. 'Can they bite us, then, even though we're stardust?'

Allegra nodded. 'We can get injured while we're stardust spirits just as easily as when we're human. Adders are the only poisonous creatures though and they mainly stay out of the woods and only bite if they feel threatened.'

'We're more likely to be a danger to

each other!' Ella grinned. 'Allegra knocked me flying with a gust of wind the other day.'

Not wanting them to start telling their stories again, Lucy hastily changed the subject. 'So what are we looking for?'

'Fish hooks caught in birds' beaks, trampled reeds, litter in the water, otter markings.'

'I'd love to see an otter,' Faye said.

They looked hard but they didn't find any. However, Allegra did point out the type of places that otters might use as their dens and they did help a duckling with its head trapped inside a discarded plastic carton. It was fun exploring the river together and then they played hide-and-seek in the trees. It was less fun when the others decided to practise using their magic powers. Lucy couldn't join in and had to just watch. She sat on a tree branch, playing with the hem of her grey dress and wishing that she knew what her powers were so she could have a go at practising too.

I want to be an autumn spirit like Allegra, she thought, watching as Allegra danced through the air and conjured a gust of wind that shook the top-most leaves of a nearby tree.

Faye and Ella clapped and Allegra bowed towards them, grinning. 'See, we *are* getting better at controlling our magic.'

'My turn now,' Ella said eagerly.

Lucy felt very left out and she was relieved when it was finally just her and Allegra on the way home.

'Do you always meet up with Faye and

Ella?' she asked as they flew back over the fields.

'Yes. Why?' Allegra said.

'Oh, nothing,' Lucy said quickly.

But on her way back to her bedroom she thought it over. She wasn't used to having a best friend she had to share and, if she was honest, she wasn't really sure she liked it. *At least Faye and Ella live quite far away*, she reasoned. *It's not like we see them in the daytime too.*

Thinking that comforting thought, she smiled. She and Allegra had already made loads of plans for how they were going to spend the rest of the school holidays. Happiness flowed through Lucy. It was going to be fun!

★

As soon as Lucy woke up the next morning, she jumped out of bed and hurried downstairs. One of the best things about stardust magic was that she never seemed to feel tired in the mornings. To her surprise, Rachel and Hope were in the kitchen getting breakfast.

'You're up early,' Lucy said.

'We've got a pony day today,' Hope explained.

Lucy understood. Rachel and Hope went riding each weekend and sometimes their riding school had special days when they got to look after a pony all day. Lucy wanted to start riding too but her mum said she had to wait until she was ten.

Just then Mrs Evans walked into the kitchen. She had the phone in her hand.

'Hi, Mum!' Lucy said. She frowned as

she realized that her mum looked worried.

Hope seemed to have noticed as well. 'What's the matter, Mum?' she asked.

'That was Richard,' Mrs Evans replied, 'Dad's friend who works on the council. He was ringing to warn us that it looks like those new houses are going to go ahead. The final decision is going to be made in four days' time but he doesn't think there have been any substantial enough objections to stop it.'

Lucy had heard her parents talking about the fact that a property developer had bought the fields behind them and was planning to build ten big houses there. She knew that they didn't want it to happen.

'So there'll be loads of bulldozers and things,' Rachel said.

'Yes,' her mum replied. 'The fields will be totally dug up.'

'But we won't be able to ride there any more,' Rachel said. 'We often go for hacks across those fields.'

'Well, you certainly won't be able to if the building work goes ahead,' Mrs Evans said. 'There'll just be houses there. Even worse, the builder's apparently planning on cutting down some of the trees. He's bought part of the woodland too. So it's not just the fields we'll lose – it's the trees as well.'

'He's going to cut down the trees!' Lucy exclaimed.

Mrs Evans nodded. 'Not all of them, of course, the woods are much too big, but the ones at the edge of the fields. Your dad's going to be so upset. You know how he used to play in those trees when he was little.'

'He found an injured dormouse there once, didn't he?' Hope said. 'And kept it as a pet.'

'He did.' Mrs Evans smiled. 'You couldn't do that now. Dormice are a protected species, it's an offence to disturb them or their homes. It's a pity the dormice left the woods. If they were still there then the developer wouldn't stand a chance getting planning permission.' She sat down at the table and sighed. 'I just wish there was something we could do to stop these houses being built.'

'Can't anything be done, Mum?' Rachel asked. 'No one wants the trees cut down.'

Mrs Evans shook her head. 'I know. But I really don't think there's any way of stopping it now. Your dad and I and other people in the village have written lots of letters but none of them have had any effect. It's such a shame. There might not be dormice in the woods now but there are lots of other animals who matter.'

Lucy felt very worried. Her mum was right. There were rabbits and squirrels, field mice and shrews – all sorts of animals. What would they do when the machines moved in? What if they fled from the woods or, even worse, got injured or killed? 'There's got to be something we can do to stop it, Mum,' she said urgently.

'I'm afraid there isn't,' Mrs Evans said, shaking her head.

There has to be something, Lucy thought quickly. *There just has to be!*

CHAPTER

Seven

Allegra was out all day with Xanthe and
so Lucy couldn't talk to her. But as soon as
they met up that night, Lucy told Allegra
what her mum had said about the housing
development.

'Apparently it's really likely to go ahead.
The trees are going to be cut down,' she
said as they landed on the decking to talk.
'It's awful, isn't it?'

'Yeah. Xanthe's been talking about it today too,' Allegra replied. 'She's been trying to think of a way to stop it happening but she hasn't had any luck yet.' She looked around. 'Well, shall we go and meet the others then?'

Lucy frowned. 'Can't we stay here tonight?' She wanted to stay and try to think of a plan to stop the development.

'Stay here?' Allegra said in surprise. 'Why?'

'Well, we can try to think of something that will save the woods,' Lucy answered.

'But if Xanthe can't think of anything, we're not going to be able to,' Allegra argued. She shook her head. 'No, let's just go and meet the others. It'll be more fun.' She flew into the air in a lightning burst of speed. 'Come on! Let's go!'

Lucy sighed. She launched herself into the sky and followed Allegra, but she was still thinking about the housing development.

As soon as they reached the clearing, Faye and Ella flew over.

Faye looked at Lucy and seemed to notice almost immediately that there was something wrong. 'What's up, Lucy?' she asked, frowning. 'You don't look very happy.'

'It's the woods,' Lucy answered. She told Faye and Ella the whole story.

'That's dreadful!' Faye exclaimed.

Ella frowned. 'Can't we stop it?'

'But how?' Lucy said.

'If I was lucky I could maybe make the soil freeze,' said Faye thoughtfully. 'But that wouldn't stop the builders for long.'

'I could make the trees and plants keep growing back but I'm sure the diggers would uproot them all in the end,' Ella said.

'I just don't think there's anything we can do,' Allegra shrugged. 'I mean, I could send a gale of wind but it would only put the builders off for a little while.' She shook her head. 'We're not powerful enough.'

'Allegra's right,' Ella agreed. 'But don't worry, Lucy, if there's anything magical that can be done, I'm sure Xanthe or one of the other stardust adults will think of it.'

'Yeah,' Allegra said. 'Stop stressing, Luce.' She grinned. 'Come on, let's play tag now!' Turning a somersault, she tagged Ella on the arm. 'You're it, Ella!' she shouted, whooshing away.

With a shriek, Ella raced after her.

Faye hesitated a moment and then followed them. 'Come on, Lucy!'

But Lucy wasn't really in the mood to play a game. She just couldn't stop thinking about the trees being cut down. Hanging around on the outskirts of the game, she watched as the others dived and shouted and laughed. Pictures of the animals who lived in the woods kept flashing through her mind. She saw them fleeing, terrified, from the bulldozers and builders. She saw their habitats destroyed. It would be awful. She couldn't believe Allegra and the others could be so unbothered about it.

There must be something we can do to help, she thought desperately. *But what?*

★

For the next three days, Lucy continued to rack her brains but she didn't come up with any ideas. She was sure that if she and Allegra really thought hard together they would be able to come up with a plan but, to her frustration, Allegra didn't seem to want to talk about it much. She just kept saying that if there was anything that could be done, Xanthe would think of it and at night-time, she seemed quite happy to check for disturbances and practise magic as normal.

'Stop worrying about it, Lucy,' she said whenever Lucy brought up the subject. But Lucy couldn't give up that easily and she felt hurt that Allegra, who was supposed to be her best friend, seemed keener to hang around with Faye and Ella than help her think of a plan.

On the night before the decision on the planning permission was going to be made, Lucy sat on her own in the fork of a beech tree, watching Allegra, Faye and Ella practise with their magic powers. As she watched, thoughts of the housing development buzzed through her brain.

'There!' Allegra said triumphantly to Ella and Faye as a breeze she had just conjured swept a patch of fallen leaves on the ground into a neat pile. 'It's not so difficult to control your magic, you just have to concentrate really hard!'

'It's my turn now!' Ella said. She looked round. 'I bet I can make that patch of bluebells flower.'

'Too easy!' Allegra protested. 'How about you make just one bluebell flower?'

'One?' Ella said. 'OK.'

Left out and on her own, Lucy felt frustration bubble up inside her. There was so little time left. How *could* the others just want to practise their magic? She leant her head against the rough trunk of the tree. *Think*, she told herself, *think hard*.

Hearing sudden laughter, she looked down. Allegra and Faye were grinning. Ella was standing beside a bluebell the size of a daffodil.

'OK, so maybe I need to concentrate more.' Ella grinned.

'Try another bluebell, Ella!' Allegra giggled.

'No, don't!' Faye exclaimed. 'You might make one grow even bigger next time!'

A wave of exasperation swept over Lucy and she flew down to Allegra's side. 'Look, why don't we go flying for a bit?' she pleaded. 'We could go to the edge of the woods and see if that gives us any ideas of ways to stop the houses being built.'

Allegra looked surprised. 'What? Now?'

Lucy nodded.

'But Faye hasn't had her go yet,' Allegra objected. 'And we're having fun.' She shook her head and turned away. 'No, we'll stay,' she said as if that decided the matter.

Hot anger flashed through Lucy. Why did they always have to do what Allegra wanted? Watching Allegra fly over to the others and start giggling over what Faye's challenge would be, her anger grew.

Allegra looked over her shoulder. 'Come on, Luce,' she called. 'Don't be a spoilsport.'

It was the last straw. Lucy's temper

snapped. 'No!' she exclaimed loudly. 'I don't want to!'

The others stared at her.

'I'm going to the edge of the woods,' she told them. 'I'm going to try and think of something to do.'

'But we're not allowed to go off on our own,' Ella protested.

'So?' Lucy said.

Allegra frowned. 'Lucy, stay here. It'll be much more fun.'

'For who?' Lucy retorted angrily and, turning, she flew off.

After a few minutes, she heard someone following her. 'Lucy! Wait!' Allegra's voice called.

But Lucy was fed up. Ignoring her friend, she flew away as fast as she could and, despite being a really good flyer,

Allegra only managed to catch up with
her near the edge of the woods.

'Lucy!' she exclaimed, diving straight in
front of her so Lucy had to pull up
sharply. 'Didn't you hear me? Why didn't
you wait?'

Lucy glared at her. 'What would've been
the point? You'd have just said you wanted
to go back to Faye and Ella. Well, I don't
want to sit around watching the three of
you practising your magic. I want to do
something about the building development.'

'But it's fun practising magic,' Allegra
protested.

'Not for me!' Anger and frustration beat
through Lucy's brain and the words
tumbled out of her. 'We're supposed to be
best friends, Allegra! But you never want
to do what I want. You just want to hang

around with Faye and Ella all the time.'

'I don't!' Allegra said, her voice rising.

'You do!' Lucy cried furiously.

'You're just being stupid!' Allegra exclaimed.

'I'm not!' Lucy shouted. She was too upset and confused to think straight. 'Oh forget it!' she cried, tears pricking her eyes as she swung round. 'I'm going!'

'No!' Allegra exclaimed, flying round in front of her.

'I'm going and you can't stop me!' Lucy yelled.

'Want to bet?' Allegra looked almost as angry as Lucy felt. 'Wind!' she shouted as Lucy started to fly away. 'Be with me!'

There was a wild whooshing sound and Lucy felt a gust of wind hit her full on. She was flung sideways. She would have cried out but all the breath had been knocked out of her. Her arms and legs flailed helplessly as the wind battered against her. Suddenly she was hurtling to the ground, out of control.

She dimly heard Allegra's panicked shriek. 'Wind be gone!'

The next instant the wind died, but it was too late – the ground was too close. Lucy just managed to turn herself round when, with a sickening thud, she hit the earth.

She lay very still, totally dazed. Her eyes were shut but the world seemed to be spinning. Was she alive? Was she dead? Her brain seemed too confused to decide.

'Lucy!' she heard Allegra's panicked voice. 'Lucy!'

Lucy felt someone shaking her arm. She

blinked her eyes open. Allegra was crouching beside her, her face full of fear and concern. 'Are you OK?'

'I . . . I think so,' Lucy managed to say.

Utter relief washed over Allegra's face. 'I thought you were dead!' she gasped. 'Oh, Lucy, I didn't mean to hurt you. I was just so angry and I wanted to stop you from leaving. I'm really, really sorry.'

'It's all right.' Lucy sat up slowly. Her bones ached but they all seemed to work. She looked round. She had landed under a chestnut tree at the edge of a clearing where thick piles of fallen leaves had broken her fall.

'Why did you try to fly away?' Allegra said. 'Why are you in such a mood with me?'

'I'm worried about the houses,' Lucy

said, but then she hesitated. If she was
honest, she knew it wasn't just that. 'And
. . . well, I guess I was also feeling left out,'
she admitted in a small voice.

'But why?' Allegra said.

'You've all got your magic powers and I
haven't,' Lucy told her. 'All I can do is sit
and watch.' Her eyes filled with tears. 'You
have so much fun with Ella and Faye,' she
mumbled. 'Sometimes I don't know
whether you're my best friend or not.'

Allegra's eyes widened. 'But I am! I
mean I really like Ella and Faye but they're
not you. I've been so happy since we've
been living next door to each other.' She
took Lucy's hand. 'I *am* your best friend. I
promise!'

Lucy felt a rush of relief.

'I . . . I thought you liked us all hanging

round together.' Allegra looked uncertain. 'I thought you were happy.'

'I am, it's just . . .' Lucy broke off as a movement behind Allegra caught her eye.

Something was pushing its way swiftly through the thick leaves. Something long and sinuous. Lucy caught a glimpse of yellow-grey and black. She frowned. It was a . . . it was a . . .

'Snake!' she gasped as an adder reared its pointed head out of the leaves right beside Allegra's foot.

The next few seconds happened in a blur. Allegra jumped. The adder's mouth opened and Lucy caught a glimpse of needle-like poisonous fangs.

'No!' she cried and almost before she knew what was happening her hands reached out in front of her. 'NO!'

Her blood seemed to tingle, an electric surge ran through her and suddenly a ball of burning fire was shooting from her fingertips straight at the snake.

Allegra gasped in alarm and flung herself to one side. The snake reared back. The fire ball missed it by about a centimetre. Turning swiftly the snake slithered away.

'Lucy! Your power!' Allegra cried. 'You can make fire! You're a summer spirit.'

A summer spirit! Lucy hardly had time to think the words before the pile of leaves where the fireball had landed burst into flames.

Lucy and Allegra both screamed. The fire leapt through the dry vegetation, the flames flickering upwards and catching the lower branches of the chestnut tree.

Lucy scrambled to her feet. The fire crackled with heat and smoke billowed towards them. Sparks flew through the air igniting the piles of leaves around them.

'Quick!' Allegra shouted. 'Quick! We've got to do something!'

CHAPTER

Eight

Fear leapt into Lucy's heart. The fire was all around them. She looked up. Sparks were flying through the air, but they could probably still make it. But then what about the trees — and the animals?

'Come on!' Allegra gasped. 'We've got to get out of here!' She flew upwards. 'We need to get help!'

Lucy had just taken off after her when

she heard a terrified squeak. She looked down. A fat golden mouse was staring around the clearing, its dark eyes wide with fear. Directly above it a branch creaked as the fire ate through the wood.

Lucy knew she should keep flying but she just couldn't bear to see the mouse killed. Diving down, she grabbed the little creature in both hands. There was a cracking noise as the branch above her began to break. Lucy darted quickly into the air. Her heart pounding, she rose up, twisting and turning to avoid the flying sparks.

What was going to happen? She'd saved this mouse but how many animals *would* be killed in the fire?

A shadow fell over her. She glanced up and stared. A dark cloud had appeared

overhead! The next second rain was
pelting down. Sheltering the mouse, Lucy
struggled through the downpour, gasping
and spluttering in surprise.

'Lucy, over here!' She heard Allegra's
voice as she reached the top of the trees
and blinked.

Allegra was flying just out of the range
of the cloud. She was with Faye and Ella!

Faye's hands were pointing at the cloud
and she had a look of intense concentration
on her face.

Shaking back her sopping hair, Lucy
flew over to them, almost crying with
relief.

'What's happening?' Ella demanded in
alarm. 'Faye and I came after you. We
weren't sure where you'd gone but then we
saw the flames and Faye used her magic to

make rain.'

'She's putting out the fire!' Allegra said in excitement. 'It's working!'

It was. As the rain fell, the flames flickered more slowly and finally died out.

'Rain be gone!' Faye murmured and the rain stopped.

Lucy flew up to her. 'Oh, Faye, thank you! You're amazing!'

'Brilliant!' Allegra and Ella agreed.

Faye looked pleased. 'I'm just glad it stopped the fire. What happened? How did it start?'

Lucy swallowed. 'It . . . it was me.'

Faye and Ella stared.

'Lucy's found her powers,' Allegra said quickly. 'She was trying to protect me. An adder tried to bite me and she sent a ball of fire at it.'

'You conjured a fireball!' Faye said to Lucy. 'You must be a really powerful summer spirit. Most summer spirits our age can only make things heat up. They can't conjure fire – even some of the adults find it difficult. How did you do it?'

'I don't know,' Lucy admitted. 'I was just so scared the snake was going to bite Allegra. I pointed my hands and suddenly it happened. It stopped the snake but then the leaves caught fire.' She looked down at the burnt clearing. A thick layer of smoke was hanging over it and there was a horrid smell of wet burnt leaves. 'Look at it. It's all my fault!'

'I wonder how much damage has been done,' Ella said, looking worried.

'I'll clear the smoke,' Allegra said. 'And then we'll be able to see.'

She pointed her hands at the clearing and concentrated hard. 'Wind, come to me!' she whispered.

A fresh breeze blew up and swept through the clearing until the smoke – and the smell – had gone.

They flew down. Lucy was horrified. The side of the clearing near where she and Allegra had been standing was blackened and charred. The plants and grass burnt to the ground. The chestnut tree they had been under had great burn marks like black scars running up its thick trunk.

As she landed, the mouse squeaked and the others noticed him for the first time.

'Is that what you went back for?' Allegra said to Lucy, looking at the mouse's nose sticking out of the crook of Lucy's arm.

Lucy nodded. 'A branch was about to fall on him. I couldn't leave him.' She tried to put the mouse down but he wouldn't leave her arms. She didn't blame him. 'OK, you can stay with me,' she said, tucking him into her pocket. She looked round the clearing, her heart sinking. 'What are we going to do? It looks dreadful. We're going to have to tell the adults, aren't we?'

'Not necessarily,' Ella replied. She was frowning thoughtfully. 'I could try to regrow things.'

'Really?' Lucy said, hope leaping inside her. 'Do you think you'd be able to?'

Ella nodded. 'If I concentrate. The problem is not letting anything grow too big.'

'Well, concentrate really hard,' Faye begged Ella. 'We don't want a glade of giant bluebells.'

Frowning intently, Ella held out her hands. 'Grow anew,' she whispered, looking round the clearing. 'Heal and grow!'

One after another the burnt trees, plants and flowers seemed to shimmer slightly.

'It's working!' Lucy gasped suddenly as a patch of burnt campion beside the trees burst upwards, the leaves green, the buds

opening into pink flowers. Bluebells grew
and opened. The scars on the chestnut tree
faded and its blackened leaves turned
green. Bit by bit, all traces of the fire disappeared and at last the glade was perfect
again.

Ella looked round as if she couldn't
believe it. 'I did it!'

'Oh, Ella!' Faye said, looking delighted
and relieved. 'You've saved the day.'

'It wasn't just me,' Ella said. 'You
stopped the fire. And Allegra got rid of the
smoke.'

'And if it hadn't been for Lucy I might
have been poisoned by the snake,' Allegra
said. 'We saved the day together – all of
us!'

The next minute they were all hugging.
As she felt the others' arms around her,

Lucy felt all her jealousy melt away in a rush of relief. Thank goodness Faye and Ella had been there!

A frantic squeaking made the four of them pull apart.

'It's the mouse!' Lucy said, remembering the tiny creature. Reaching into her pocket, she cupped her hands round the mouse. His black nose stuck up between Lucy's thumbs, his long whiskers twitching in alarm. 'Did you think you were going to be squashed?' Lucy said to him. She crouched down. 'Well, you can go back down now. It's all beautiful again.' She released him. He looked round for a moment, his chestnut-gold fur glimmering in the starlight.

'Lucy!' Allegra gasped. 'That's not an ordinary mouse. It . . . it's a dormouse!'

Lucy stared at the plump mouse with his long bushy tail. 'A dormouse?'

'Yes!' Allegra said.

The dormouse scampered across the grass and jumped on to a fallen branch. He hurried along it, heading towards a grove of hazel trees at the far side of the clearing.

'Come on, let's follow him and see if there are any more,' Allegra said.

They flew up into the air and followed the dormouse towards the hazel trees. He jumped off the branch, rustled through some leaves and then hopped on to an old fallen tree trunk. Halfway along it, he stopped and dived off. They saw him run across the ground towards the nearest hazel tree. Reaching it, he scurried about a foot up the trunk and disappeared.

Lucy flew closer. Reaching the tree she saw there was a loose nest made out of grass and leaves in a fork in the lower branches. It looked sort of like a bird's nest but almost completely round with just a hole in the top. She saw the tip of the dormouse's long bushy tail vanishing inside.

'He's got a nest,' she said to the others. She began to look round at the nearby hazel bushes. There was another nest – and another!

'Look!' she cried. 'There're lots of them!'

'I bet these must be the nuts they have been eating,' Ella said, picking up an old hazelnut shell from the ground. A neat round hole had been gnawed at the top.

'I wonder when they came back,' Ella said. 'We should have noticed.'

'I suppose we don't normally come this close to the edge of the woods,' Faye put in.

'I can't wait to tell my mum!' Allegra said. 'I know she's been really hoping the dormice would come back.'

'My dad will be pleased too,' Lucy said. 'When he was little, he used to watch the dormice in the woods and he even had one as a pet.' As she spoke, a memory tugged at a corner of her mind. She frowned. She had a feeling there was some other reason why finding dormice was important. What was it?

'We'll have to look after them,' Faye said. 'Dormice are really rare. It's a pity they've chosen to nest so close to the edge of the woods though,' she said looking to the left where the woods ended and the fields began. 'It's going to be harder to protect them from people here.'

'Oh no,' Allegra shrieked.

The others looked at her.

'What about the builders! The new

houses are going to be built just over there. What about the noise and the machines?'

As she spoke, the memory that Lucy had been groping for suddenly popped into her mind. She gasped. *Of course!*

'Oh my goodness!' Ella exclaimed. 'The poor dormice! They'll hate it!'

'What if they leave again? This is awful!' Faye cried.

'Oh no it isn't!' Lucy exclaimed, her eyes shining with delight.

The others looked at her in astonishment. 'What do you mean?' Allegra said. 'Of course it's awful!'

'No, don't you see?' Lucy's face broke into a huge grin. 'This is the perfect solution!'

Nine

Allegra, Ella and Faye stared at Lucy as if she were mad.

'What do you mean, the perfect solution?' Allegra demanded. 'How can it be? Dormice hate noise and disturbance. They'll leave as soon as the building work starts.'

'But it's not going to start!' Lucy said. 'My mum said that if there were still dormice in the woods then the builder wouldn't be able to get the planning permission he needed and he wouldn't be allowed to build the houses.'

Allegra's eyes widened. 'So if we tell people about the dormice in the morning then the houses won't be built?'

Lucy nodded. 'But we'll have to tell them tomorrow. That's when the decision's being made.'

'Oh, Lucy!' Allegra shrieked. 'You're brilliant!' She flew over and hugged her. 'You've thought of a way to save the woods! You're amazing!'

'A genius!' Ella cried.

'Totally,' Faye agreed. 'Oh, Lucy. This is perfect and we'd never have found out if it hadn't been for you!'

Looking round at their delighted faces,

Lucy felt suddenly very happy. How could she ever have wished it was just her and Allegra? Having three friends to celebrate with was so much better than just having one!

They flew back to the secret glade. Xanthe confirmed what Lucy's mum had said. 'Dormice are a protected species. It's an offence to disturb them or their homes in any way. I'll ring the planning officer in the morning. There's no way the planning permission will be granted.' She looked round curiously at them all. 'How did you find the dormice? They're such shy creatures. It's really unusual to see them.'

'It was Lucy,' Faye said. 'She found one when she discovered her powers.'

'You've discovered your powers?'

Xanthe looked at Lucy in surprise.

Lucy nodded. 'I'm a summer spirit,' she said.

'Really? How did you find that out?' Xanthe asked.

'I . . . er . . . I just did,' Lucy said hastily.

Xanthe gave her a quizzical look. But to Lucy's relief she seemed to decide it was wisest not to ask for more details. 'Well, I'm very glad,' she said, smiling. 'So have you seen your star yet?'

'No,' Lucy said eagerly.

Xanthe turned to the south and walked a few paces away. She beckoned Lucy over. 'There,' she said, pointing upwards. 'It's called Regulus – the summer star – and it's part of the lion constellation. Can you see it? It's just to the right and –'

'I can see it,' Lucy interrupted quietly.

She stared at the bright star overhead. It was as if all the other stars in the sky had faded. As she gazed at Regulus, power seemed to surge through her and her fingertips tingled hotly. Almost without realizing what she was doing, she clenched her hands.

'It's pulling me to it,' she breathed, feeling a current flowing between her and her star.

'That's the flow of magic,' Xanthe told her. 'The sharing of power between star and stardust spirit. You will have to learn how to use that power, Lucy – how to use it wisely and well.' Lucy heard a note of warning in Xanthe's voice and looked at her. 'Summer spirits are strong and often very powerful,' Xanthe went on softly, her eyes suddenly very serious. 'You must make sure you use your power for good.'

'I will,' Lucy whispered.

She turned back to look at Regulus. Every inch of her body seemed to glow. She smiled. At long last, she had found her star!

The next morning, Lucy went round to Allegra's house straight after breakfast. At nine o'clock, Xanthe rang the council and reported the dormice.

'They're sending someone over to investigate right away,' she smiled when she eventually put the phone down. 'The man said that if dormice are nesting there then there's no way planning permission will be granted for those fields. In fact the woods will become a protected site.'

Lucy was so delighted that she ran

straight home to tell her family.

'But that means the builder won't be allowed to develop the land,' Mrs Evans said.

'I know!' Lucy said.

'So the trees won't be cut down!' Rachel exclaimed. For one moment, Lucy almost thought Rachel was actually going to hug her. But then at the last minute her sister seemed to think better of it. 'That's brilliant!' she declared, sitting down.

'They really won't be able to build the houses?' Hope said to their mum.

Mrs Evans smiled. 'No.'

Hope, Rachel and Lucy exchanged smiles of relief.

At three o'clock the news came through from Xanthe. The planning permission for

the housing development had been turned
down. The fields and the trees were safe.

'I still can't believe it,' Lucy said as she
and Allegra sat on the wooden decking
later that evening and watched the sun go
down.

'It's wonderful,' Allegra said, taking a sip
of fairy lemonade. 'The animals and trees
are safe and we have dormice to help look
after. Also, Xanthe says that maybe if the
dormice have started coming back some of
the other rare animals and birds might too.'

'We'll have to work really hard to keep
the woods perfect for them,' Lucy declared.
Her eyes glowed as she imagined the forest
filling up with some of the rare animals she
had heard Xanthe talk about – otters, large
blue butterflies, firecrests . . . It would be
wonderful!

'We can use our powers and do it together . . .' Allegra broke off, a worried look crossing her face and Lucy was sure she was remembering the argument the night before.

She smiled. 'Yes, together — you, me, Ella and Faye.'

Allegra grinned in delight.

'The sun's set,' Lucy said quickly. 'Let's go to the woods!'

Allegra grabbed her hands and together they looked into the sky and said, 'I believe in stardust, I believe in stardust, *I believe in stardust!*'

Lucy felt the familiar dissolving feeling and the next minute she was shooting up into the sky.

'Your clothes!' Allegra exclaimed.

Lucy looked down. 'Oh wow!' she

gasped. Her dress was no longer pearly grey but a glowing, shimmering gold.

'It's because you've found your star!' Allegra said. 'You're a real stardust spirit now!'

Lucy spun round in the air. The dress swirled around her, glittering and beautiful. Looking up, Lucy saw Regulus shining in the sky. Power tingled through every cell of her body and for a moment she thought she was going to burst with happiness.

'Come on!' Allegra shouted. 'Let's go and show the others your new dress.'

Shooting one last smile at Regulus, Lucy dived after her and they flew off through the starry sky.